To Vicki, for all your hard work and support - M.C.

For Daisy and Oliver Ramsbotham - S.G.

A TEMPLAR BOOK

First published in 2011 by Templar Publishing,
an imprint of The Templar Company Limited,
The Granary, Dorking, Surrey, RH4 1DN, UK
www.templarco.co.uk

1 3 5 7 9 8 6 4 2

ISBN 978-1-84877-408-7

Concept by A.J. Wood
Design by Tracey Cunnell

Printed in China

Rabbit and the Big Red Scooter

Stella Gurney

Illustrated by Mark Chambers

templar publishing

Rabbit trundled everywhere on his little blue tricycle.
He loved to pedal along with the wind in his ears
and a song in his heart.

"Cooee, Caterpillar!"

Everyone was always pleased to see Rabbit.

"Hello, Voley!"

"Mercy me, Mouse. Those bags look heavy – hop on."

He always had time for a chat or to lend a friend a helping hand.

Then one day, Hare rocked into town.
You could hear his big green scooter long before you saw it.
It skidded to a halt alongside Rabbit, sending up a cloud of dust.

"That's a lovely, shiny
new scooter!" said Rabbit,
trying not to sneeze.

"Isn't it?" replied Hare. "With a scooter you're King of the Road."

After that, Rabbit's tricycle didn't seem quite so good.
For the first time, he noticed that the paint was flaking and the
wheels squeaked. Even his saddlebags had lost their magic.

And no matter how hard he pedalled,
his tricycle never went fast enough.

Then one day, something in the window of his favourite shop caught Rabbit's eye.

It was **BIG**...

it was **RED**...

it was **SHINY.**

"COo-ool!"
breathed Rabbit.

He had to have it.

Minutes later, Rabbit was standing outside, the proud owner of a brand new scooter.

BERT's BIKES
MEAN MACHINES
FOR MACHO MAMMALS

"Is that yours?" asked Frog.
"Obviously," said Rabbit.

"It looks a bit big," said Mouse.

"Nonsense," snapped Rabbit. "On this, I'm going to be King of the Road!"

"Are you going to ride it now, Rabbit?" asked Bear.

"Absolutely," said Rabbit.

Rabbit's friends watched as he tried to start the engine.

Finally, it sparked into life with a **tremendous roar.**

The big red scooter sprang forward and then shot off down the road.

"Watch out, ducks!"

Soon, Rabbit could be seen roaring up and down the High Street every day on his big shiny new scooter.

It was a bit of a handful, but he felt better once he'd bought a fancy new biker jacket and some goggles. He thought he looked pretty cool... his friends weren't so sure.

"Can't stop now, Voley!"

These days, he wasn't kind or helpful like the old Rabbit.

"Out of my way, Mouse!"

And then, something awful happened.

It had been raining all week

BUS

and the road was **Wet and slippery.**

Rabbit spotted Hare up ahead and decided to show him who was King of the Road.

He sped up to overtake him...

but things didn't go...

quite as Rabbit had planned.

Smelly Dung!

After that, Rabbit decided to put the big red scooter up for sale.
Truth be told, the seat had chafed him dreadfully
and the helmet had bent his ears.

But most of all,
zooming around so fast, Rabbit
hadn't had time to speak to his friends.

Later that week, Rabbit was rummaging around in his garage, looking for ways to be handy when he spotted his old trike.

KEEP OFF! except for Rabbit...

CARROT

COMPOST

What a beautiful thing it was!

Rabbit couldn't help himself. He wheeled the trike out into his driveway and set to work.

After that, everything pretty much returned to normal.

Except on Sundays...

when Rabbit found a new way to be

King of the Road!